Living Life

Haters And Judg
Gu

By
Valerie White

Copyright © 2024 All Rights Reserved.

Table of Contents

Chapter 1
Living My Best Life: Senior Year 5

Chapter 2
Seeing Both Sides of the World 12

Chapter 3
Defying Stereotypes 18

Chapter 4
The Pain of Loss 27

Chapter 5
Destiny and Determination 35

Chapter 6
Understanding and Venting 45

Chapter 7
Encountering the Unexpected 53

Chapter 8
Growing Up and Moving On 63

Chapter 9
Friends and Fun Times 69

Chapter 10
Staying True to Yourself 76

Living life is hard enough, but living life among haters is a whole other adventure.

The mere thought of the word "haters" upsets people to the point of having to explain one's opinions. It makes you wonder what makes you a hater or why that word gets attached to people.

Let me explain my opinion:

Chapter 1
Living My Best Life: Senior Year

The word "haters" often evokes a strong emotional response, serving as a catch-all term for those who criticize or judge us, sometimes without a full understanding of our circumstances. It simplifies the multifaceted nature of judgment, reducing it to a monolithic concept that can be both overwhelming and misinterpreted. This term can amplify feelings of resentment or insecurity, as it implies a broad and often unjust hostility toward us. To grasp why this word and its implications impact us so profoundly, it's essential to delve deeper into the nuances of judgment and its role in personal development. Allow me to recount my own journey, shedding light on how I navigated the complexities of external criticism and learned to harness these experiences for personal growth and self-improvement.

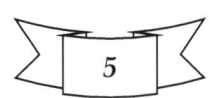

It all started in the year 1993. This was the year Bill Clinton was the President of the United States, and the end of Desert Storm, the most talked-about war, dominated the news. It was also the year I became acutely aware that life had become an open arena for people to judge and criticize. This year stood out as a crucible of both triumph and challenge, shaping my high school journey in ways that would have lasting effects on my sense of identity and resilience. The trials and successes I encountered during this pivotal period were instrumental in defining who I would become, setting the stage for my personal growth and the broader lessons I would carry forward. As a senior at Crim High School in 1993, my path to graduation was far from straightforward. I had initially been a student at Southside High, where I was on track to graduate in the spring of 1992. However, a scheduling error emerged that left me just half an hour short of the required credits for graduation. This seemingly minor discrepancy, though numerically insignificant, had significant implications for my academic journey. It meant that I had to remain enrolled for an additional year at Crim High to complete the necessary coursework and secure my diploma. Although this extension of my high school experience was unexpected and initially disheartening, it was also a period that tested my determination and perseverance. I refused to let this setback derail my plans. My commitment to earning my diploma remained steadfast, and I approached my final year with a renewed sense of purpose and resolve, determined to overcome the administrative hurdles and finish what I had started.

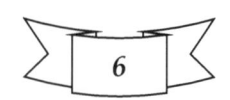

Living with my boyfriend, who was eight years my senior, significantly impacted my high school experience, adding a complex and sometimes contentious layer to my life. Our relationship, marked by this age difference, drew considerable scrutiny and judgment from those around us. Many questioned the appropriateness and future of our partnership, expressing concerns about the age gap and what it might imply. Their judgments were rooted in the conventional norms of the early 1990s, which often did not accommodate such unconventional arrangements. Despite this, our relationship provided me with a crucial source of support and stability during a tumultuous time. He was not merely a figure in my life but a steadfast partner who played a vital role in my personal development. His encouragement was instrumental in helping me remain focused on my education and career aspirations. He actively supported me through the challenges I faced, offering both practical and emotional support. Our living situation was far from just a shared space; it was a dynamic partnership where we both learned, grew, and mutually reinforced our ambitions. His presence was a stabilizing force, enabling me to navigate the uncertainties of my senior year with greater confidence and determination.

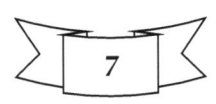

High school during that period was a tumultuous whirlwind of experiences and emotions, each day bringing its own set of challenges and revelations. I had recently acquired my own car, a significant symbol of independence and autonomy that allowed me to manage my own schedule and navigate the demands of teenage life with a newfound freedom. This personal achievement was both empowering and emblematic of my desire to take control of my future. Alongside this newfound independence, I was grappling with the complexities of teenage life, a process that was further complicated by my unique circumstances. My decisions, such as living with an older boyfriend and transferring school's mid-way through my high school career, frequently became subjects of scrutiny and criticism from peers and adults alike. These choices, while deeply personal and reflective of my own journey, often clashed with conventional expectations and norms. The judgments I faced were not always empathetic or understanding, adding a layer of pressure and external conflict to my already challenging high school experience. However, this relentless scrutiny, though harsh at times, served as a powerful motivator. It spurred me to prove myself, demonstrating resilience and dedication in the face of adversity. I remained steadfastly committed to my education, determined to overcome the obstacles and skepticism that accompanied my unconventional path.

One particularly striking example of societal judgment that I encountered was the intense scrutiny surrounding personal choices and fashion. I vividly recall how comments about my shoes or overall appearance became a focal point for others, as if these superficial aspects were somehow indicative of my character or worth. Although these judgments might have seemed trivial at the time, they were emblematic of a broader pattern of evaluation based on external appearances rather than personal substance. This tendency to judge based on superficial details was not limited to everyday individuals but extended to well-known public figures as well. For instance, even someone as accomplished and revered as Michael Jordan faced relentless scrutiny over his fashion choices and personal style. The constant media and public focus on his appearance and preferences illustrated that judgment is a pervasive aspect of life, affecting people across all walks of society. Observing this phenomenon highlighted to me that judgment, while often seemingly petty or unwarranted, is a common experience shared by many. It underscored the reality that navigating judgment is an intrinsic part of the human experience, regardless of one's status or achievements.

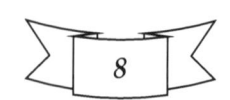

The necessity of staying an extra year to complete my high school graduation was a profound test of my perseverance and resolve. At the time, this additional year felt like a monumental challenge rather than a minor setback. The mix of emotions I experienced was intense: I was frustrated by the delay and the administrative error that had extended my high school career, but I was also deeply determined to overcome this hurdle. Knowing that I had to earn a few more credits to secure my diploma, I approached this final year with a focused commitment to my goal. Each day of that extended year was marked by a relentless pursuit of academic and personal milestones, as I worked diligently to meet the requirements necessary for graduation. Despite the inconvenience and the feeling of being out of sync with my original graduating class, I remained steadfast in my goal to graduate alongside my peers. The culmination of this effort came with the graduation ceremony, a moment of profound significance and pride. Walking across the stage to receive my diploma, with my family cheering and celebrating my achievement from the audience, was an emotionally charged experience. It was not just a personal triumph but a public affirmation of my ability to surmount obstacles and prove my resilience. This moment underscored the fact that despite the challenges and delays, I had successfully navigated the difficulties and achieved my goal, affirming my capability to overcome adversity and fulfill my ambitions.

In retrospect, my high school years emerged as a pivotal period of growth and self-discovery, marked by both profound challenges and significant personal development. This period was not merely a phase of academic learning but also a transformative journey where I learned to navigate the complex landscape of judgment and criticism that surrounded me. Each encounter with criticism, whether related to my personal choices, fashion, or lifestyle, presented an opportunity for me to build resilience and refine my understanding of myself. I became adept at filtering out unconstructive feedback and honing my ability to stay laser-focused on my goals despite the external noise. This was crucial in maintaining my commitment to my academic and personal aspirations. Alongside this, I learned to embrace and deeply value the support and encouragement from those who believed in me. The positive reinforcement and understanding from these individuals were instrumental in sustaining my motivation and bolstering my confidence. The challenges I encountered, ranging from navigating academic hurdles to dealing with societal judgments and misconceptions, played a significant role in shaping my character and perspective. These experiences collectively contributed to my development, teaching me important life skills such as perseverance, self-reliance, and the ability to remain steadfast in the face of adversity. Looking back, I recognize that these formative years laid the foundation for who I am today, having profoundly influenced my approach to life and my ability to handle future challenges with grace and determination.

When we discuss the concept of "haters" and the judgments we encounter, it's important to recognize that these elements are integral parts of the larger tapestry of life. While they can undoubtedly be challenging and often feel overwhelming, they also present valuable opportunities for personal growth and the development of resilience. Facing criticism and judgment is not just a test of endurance but also a chance to cultivate a deeper understanding of oneself and to build inner strength. Rather than allowing the opinions and judgments of others to dictate your sense of worth or undermine your self-confidence, it is crucial to maintain a focus on your own goals and the supportive relationships that bolster your journey. For me, navigating my senior year was a multifaceted experience that went beyond simply surviving the academic and social pressures. It involved fully embracing my authentic self, confronting and overcoming various obstacles, and finding joy in the process of achieving my milestones. This period was about recognizing my own value and capability, despite the external criticisms, and celebrating the personal victories that came from staying true to my goals and aspirations. By focusing on my own growth and the positive support I received, I was able to transform these challenges into stepping stones toward a more fulfilling and self-assured life.

Chapter 2
Seeing Both Sides of the World

This is Lady V, the youngest of six siblings. My life began in what many would call a chaotic and dysfunctional family, but I'm not here to point fingers or dwell on the past. Let's start from the beginning. My father had a rather unconventional lifestyle, being married to three different women at the same time, each with their own set of children by him. Yes, it sounds wild, but that was my reality, the norm I grew up with. My mother had her own unique journey before meeting my father. She had two children from previous relationships—one with a married man, which brought its own set of complications, and another with a man who was a pimp, whose identity remained a mystery to everyone. Together, they had my sister and me, adding to our already blended and diverse family dynamic. It's easy to think of this as a tumultuous upbringing, and in many ways, it was. But I believe there's a higher purpose to it all. I firmly hold onto the faith that God placed me in this family for a reason, and as the saying goes, He doesn't make mistakes. This belief has been my anchor through the ups and downs, and it shapes how I view my past and present.

Growing up in such a complex family structure was anything but straightforward. My father's multiple marriages created a tangled web of relationships, with each wife and set of siblings contributing to the intricate dynamics. The situation often felt like a puzzle with too many pieces, each one representing a different aspect of my life. My mother's past only added to the complexity, with her previous relationships bringing their own stories and challenges into the mix. Despite the dysfunction that surrounded us, my parents managed to show me both sides of the world—the good and the bad.

From them, I learned valuable lessons about resilience and the importance of being vigilant in every situation. They taught me to always be aware of my surroundings, a skill that became crucial as I navigated the complex social landscape of high school. They also instilled in me the importance of perseverance and the necessity of finishing what I started, no matter how tough things got. These lessons became especially important during my senior year, a pivotal time when I was preparing to transition into adulthood. It was a period filled with challenges and self-discovery, but the foundation laid by my parents' teachings helped me find my way through. Their guidance, though often unconventional, provided me with a unique perspective on life, one that has shaped who I am today.

My senior year marked a pivotal moment in my life, filled with both excitement and uncertainty. I transferred to a new school, leaving behind the familiar faces, routines, and comfort of my previous environment. This transition presented me with a fresh start, a blank slate where I could reinvent myself and explore new opportunities. At the time, I was living with my older boyfriend, a decision that set me apart from many of my peers. It was an unconventional arrangement, one that often drew curious glances and whispered judgments, but it was my reality and a significant aspect of my journey. Our relationship was more than just companionship; it was a defining force that influenced many of my decisions and perspectives. We faced numerous challenges together, from managing household responsibilities to navigating the complexities of our age difference. Despite the obstacles, we provided unwavering support to each other, forming a bond that felt unbreakable. This relationship played a crucial role in shaping my experiences and growth during this transformative period of my life.

During my senior year, one of the most challenging aspects was navigating the constant stream of judgments and expectations from those around me. People were quick to voice their opinions about my family, my choice to live with an older boyfriend, and the decisions I made regarding my future. In that era, societal judgments were pervasive, and it seemed like everyone felt entitled to offer their unsolicited opinions. The term "haters" wasn't widely used back then, but the sentiment was unmistakable. The whispers and side glances were constant reminders that I was being scrutinized for my choices, which often didn't align with the conventional norms of the time. Despite the pressure and negativity, I refused to let others' perceptions dictate my path. I learned the importance of resilience and staying true to myself, focusing on my personal goals and aspirations rather than the opinions of those who didn't understand my journey.

In the 90s, teen pregnancy was a prevalent issue, particularly in my community and among the girls in my family and school. It wasn't uncommon to see young mothers balancing their studies with childcare responsibilities. Our high school even had a daycare center specifically for teen moms, which was considered a typical response to the situation at the time. Despite the normalization of this reality, I was determined not to follow that path. Observing the challenges faced by my peers who became mothers at a young age, I resolved to avoid the same fate. I set my mind on finishing school without the added responsibility of a child, knowing that achieving my educational goals would open up more opportunities for my future. This commitment was a personal goal that I took very seriously, and it required me to make careful decisions and maintain a strong focus on my studies and long-term aspirations.

My faith has been a cornerstone in my life, profoundly influencing my decisions and outlook. I always made a conscious effort to put God first, seeking guidance through prayer and reflection, especially during challenging times. This spiritual foundation provided me with the strength and clarity needed to navigate the complexities of my family dynamics and relationships. Each family member, with their unique personalities and quirks, played a significant role in shaping my character and values. Through our interactions, I learned invaluable lessons about resilience, the importance of persevering in the face of adversity, and the necessity of thoughtful consideration before acting. These experiences not only deepened my faith but also instilled in me a sense of gratitude and humility, reminding me of the importance of empathy and understanding in all aspects of life.

Reflecting on my experiences growing up, I realize they profoundly shaped my understanding of the world and my approach to life. I learned early on that entering difficult situations often seems deceptively easy, but extricating oneself from them can be far more challenging and fraught with complications. These formative years were filled with moments where my decisions led me into complex predicaments, each one serving as a powerful lesson in the importance of caution and deliberate thoughtfulness. I became acutely aware of how my actions could have far-reaching consequences, fostering a deep sense of responsibility in me. Despite the obstacles and hardships, I faced, I hold a deep sense of gratitude for these experiences. They were pivotal in molding my character, teaching me resilience, and guiding me towards becoming the person I am today. Each challenge, while difficult in the moment, contributed to my growth and equipped me with valuable insights that continue to influence my decisions and outlook on life.

Reflecting on the past, I am transported to a time when life seemed much simpler. I recall the days when a quarter was the key to making a phone call from a payphone, and the skill of memorizing street signs was a necessity for navigating unfamiliar areas. These seemingly small details are poignant reminders of how significantly the world has transformed over the years. They underscore the importance of remaining grounded in our origins and valuing the journey that has shaped us.

As I pen this book, my intention is to convey these nostalgic experiences and the lessons they impart. My narrative is woven with themes of resilience, unwavering faith, and the critical importance of remaining true to oneself amidst change. It serves as a testament to the idea that regardless of where one begins, there exists an inherent power within to influence and shape one's own future.

Through sharing my story, I aim to inspire others to recognize their own potential and to appreciate the path that has led them to where they are today.

Navigating a complex family dynamic during my transformative senior year of high school was a journey fraught with challenges and growth. It was a period marked by facing external judgments and defying societal expectations, all while striving to stay true to my core values. The experience was not just about overcoming obstacles but also about understanding and appreciating the role my family and faith played in shaping my perspective.

Every challenge I encountered was a lesson in resilience and self-discovery. I learned to value the lessons taught by my family and the guidance provided by my faith, which became my anchors amid the turbulence. These experiences shaped my approach to life, teaching me the importance of appreciating my past and remaining steadfast in my goals.

Embracing my unique journey has become integral to living my best life. It's about acknowledging the person I've become, honoring my past, and continuing to push forward with determination and authenticity.

Chapter 3
Defying Stereotypes

The early 1990s were a period marked by dramatic contrasts and rapidly changing social norms. As I maneuvered through the intricacies of my senior year in high school, I found myself in the midst of a cultural transition that was both exhilarating and challenging. The era was defined by its vibrant pop culture, evolving fashion trends, and the burgeoning influence of technology, all of which clashed with the more traditional expectations held by society and my own family. Amidst this backdrop, I grappled with the weight of societal stereotypes and peer pressures that sought to dictate my path. My personal journey was a testament to my relentless effort to challenge and surpass these predefined expectations. Each day presented a new struggle to assert my individuality and carve out a space where I could thrive on my own terms, all while confronting the judgments and constraints imposed by those around me. The experience was not merely about overcoming obstacles but about redefining my identity in a world that was in flux.

Growing up during the vibrant and tumultuous years of the baby boom era, the societal pressure to conform to prevailing norms was a constant and often overwhelming force. Media outlets frequently highlighted teenage pregnancies, showcasing them as a common outcome for young women, which created a pervasive narrative that early motherhood was almost an inevitable part of the female adolescent experience. These portrayals, often sensationalized and devoid of nuance, suggested that girls like me were destined to follow a predetermined path of limited ambitions and early domesticity. Each day felt like a battle against the tide of these expectations, with the world seemingly conspiring to ensure that I would become just another statistic in a troubling trend. The weight of these societal pressures was palpable, and it seemed as though the broader culture was systematically aligning itself to push me into a mold that I desperately sought to escape.

In 1992, I confronted a defining moment in my life that reshaped my perspective: I came to see life as a vast, intricate canvas, and I alone wielded the brush. This realization struck me with profound clarity, marking the beginning of a crucial chapter where I was empowered to craft my future according to my own vision. Amidst the rollercoaster of triumphs and trials that life relentlessly presented, I resolved to navigate away from the limiting stereotypes that threatened to confine me. The experiences of friends and relatives who had succumbed to the burdens of early adulthood and motherhood served as stark reminders of the pitfalls I sought to avoid. Witnessing their struggles underscored my commitment to breaking free from the constraints of conventional expectations. With unwavering determination, I embraced the challenge of graduating and forging a path that diverged from the one traditionally expected of me. This resolve became both my shield against the pressures of conformity and my weapon in the pursuit of a future defined by my own choices and aspirations.

I recalled my parents' lessons from my childhood with striking clarity—particularly the numerous times they drove me around town, turning ordinary car rides into educational moments. I remember how they would quiz me on street names and landmarks, turning navigation into a game that sharpened my sense of direction. They emphasized the importance of always carrying a quarter for emergencies, a practice rooted in the necessity of pay phones, which were once as ubiquitous as they were vital. Back then, a simple quarter could be the key to making an urgent call if needed.

Today, as I navigate a world where cell phones have replaced pay phones and the need to keep our devices charged has become paramount, the essence of that lesson remains just as relevant. The shift in technology does not diminish the importance of preparedness and resourcefulness. If anything, it underscores how these fundamental qualities transcend the tools we use. Those seemingly mundane lessons about street names and emergency quarters were imbued with a deeper wisdom—an awareness of the importance of being prepared and resourceful in any situation. As I reflect on these teachings, I realize they have profoundly shaped my approach to life's challenges, illustrating how foundational lessons can have lasting impact.

As I faced the reality of my senior year, I was engulfed in a whirlwind of self-doubt and introspection. The pressure to conform to societal norms was overwhelming, a constant reminder that fitting into a predefined mold was not just expected but demanded. The very fabric of my daily interactions was woven with questions that felt like they were designed to peel back layers of my identity and expose me for scrutiny.

In conversations with both peers and adults, I encountered a barrage of questions that seemed to serve more as probes than as genuine inquiries: "What's your name?" was not just a simple introduction but a way to categorize me within their understanding of social hierarchies. "What are your aspirations?" felt like a test of my ambition, challenging whether my dreams aligned with the conventional pathways to success. "What does your family think about your future?" seemed to delve into my background, as if my family's opinions could either validate or undermine my choices.

These questions went beyond mere curiosities. They were loaded with unspoken implications, subtly pressuring me to conform to an external set of expectations. Each inquiry was a subtle challenge to assert my individuality in a world that seemed determined to impose its own standards. It felt as if my responses were being measured against an invisible yardstick, and every answer I gave was scrutinized, dissected, and often found wanting in the eyes of those who sought to fit me into a preordained narrative. In this environment, asserting my own identity felt like a radical act, one that required constant vigilance and resilience against a backdrop of societal expectations eager to shape me into something I was not.

I found a profound sense of solace in the realization that, despite my family's well-intentioned yet frequently misguided beliefs and opinions, they had inadvertently endowed me with invaluable traits of self-reliance and critical thinking. From an early age, my upbringing was characterized by a blend of rigorous expectations and sometimes misdirected advice, which, while challenging, became the bedrock of my personal development. The constant pressure to forge my own path amidst their conflicting perspectives taught me the vital importance of standing resolutely for my own convictions, even when faced with dissent. I learned to meticulously analyze situations, weigh evidence, and make informed decisions, rather than relying solely on the perspectives of others. This foundation of resilience, cultivated through navigating their expectations and embracing the inevitable uncertainties of life, has been instrumental in my ability to pursue and achieve my aspirations. Without these lessons, the complexities and challenges inherent in chasing my own goals would have been insurmountable. The experience of reconciling their influence with my own evolving identity has ultimately prepared me to confront and overcome the myriad obstacles that arise in the pursuit of my dreams.

The transition from my previous school to the new one marked a significant turning point in my life, embodying a period of intense uncertainty and profound self-discovery. As I left behind the familiar surroundings, routines, and friendships that had defined my high school experience up until that point, I was thrust into an environment that was both physically and emotionally different from what I was used to.

The new school presented a fresh set of challenges, starting with its distinct academic demands. I faced a different curriculum that required me to quickly adapt to new teaching styles, subjects, and expectations. Each classroom was a new battleground for academic success, and I had to recalibrate my study habits and strategies to keep up with the rigorous coursework. This meant long nights of studying, learning to prioritize tasks, and developing new organizational skills to manage the increased workload.

Socially, the transition was equally daunting. I walked into a new social ecosystem where I was unknown and had to navigate a complex web of established cliques, new faces, and shifting social dynamics. The challenge was not just about making new friends, but also about finding my place in this new community, understanding the social norms, and building relationships from scratch. I had to learn the art of small talk, understand the unspoken rules of social interactions, and find common ground with peers who had their own established friendships and group dynamics.

This experience also forced me to confront and reevaluate my own priorities and identity. I was no longer defined by the old labels and associations that came with my previous school; I had to discover who I was in this new context. The change required me to be introspective, to question what was truly important to me, and to redefine my goals and aspirations in light of the new challenges and opportunities before me.

The transition was a stark reminder that personal growth often demands stepping out of one's comfort zone and embracing the unknown. It highlighted that adapting to new circumstances requires resilience, flexibility, and a willingness to face and overcome the discomfort that comes with significant change. Through this period of upheaval, I learned valuable lessons about perseverance, self-reliance, and the courage to forge ahead despite uncertainty.

Reflecting on the technological advancements of the era, the contrast between the early 90s and today is striking. In 1992, accessing information was a labor-intensive process. Students relied heavily on physical resources such as libraries, where research involved sifting through stacks of books, encyclopedias, and microfiche. Index cards and handwritten notes were common tools for organizing information, and tracking down sources required perseverance and patience. The process of discovery was deliberate, often demanding hours of manual effort to piece together fragments of knowledge.

Fast forward to the present day, and the landscape has transformed dramatically. Modern students are armed with digital tools that provide instantaneous access to a vast ocean of information. With just a few clicks, they can retrieve data, consult academic journals, and even engage in interactive learning experiences online. This ease of access has revolutionized the way we approach research and learning, making information more readily available than ever before.

Yet, as I reflect on these changes, I can't help but feel that the manual effort of my generation fostered a unique appreciation for the value of information. The slow, methodical process of gathering and verifying facts imbued us with a deeper understanding of the research process and the effort required to uncover knowledge. There was a certain satisfaction in manually sorting through information and arriving at conclusions through personal diligence. This experience not only enhanced our problem-solving skills but also instilled a profound respect for the intellectual labor behind information acquisition and discovery.

The resilience and adaptability I cultivated during this formative period have proven to be invaluable throughout my life. Facing numerous challenges and changes head-on, I learned to navigate uncertainty with a positive outlook and a flexible mindset. This experience taught me not only to accept change but to actively seek out opportunities for growth and self-improvement. Each hurdle I encountered, whether in the classroom or in everyday life, reinforced my commitment to maintaining a steadfast sense of integrity and authenticity. These core values, which were deeply influenced by my diverse experiences and the lessons I gleaned from them, have become fundamental to my identity. They have guided me through complex situations, informed my decisions, and shaped my interactions with others, forming the bedrock of who I am today.

In essence, defying stereotypes involved more than merely resisting societal expectations; it was fundamentally about asserting my own unique narrative and making choices that genuinely reflected my authentic self. This process was not a one-time event but an ongoing journey, particularly as I transitioned from high school into adulthood. Each step of this journey was characterized by a constant struggle to reconcile the often-conflicting demands of external pressures with my personal aspirations and values.

Navigating this delicate balance required me to confront and question prevailing norms and prejudices, which often tried to dictate how I should live my life or define my identity. It meant challenging entrenched assumptions about who I was supposed to be and instead, forging a path that was true to my own vision of myself. Through this arduous process, I came to understand a profound truth: while the world may present a myriad of paths, opportunities, and expectations, the ultimate power to choose and define my own destiny rests firmly within my grasp. This realization empowered me to embrace my individuality and take ownership of my life's direction, regardless of external influences.

Chapter 4
The Pain of Loss

As I mentioned earlier, I come from a vibrant and bustling family, each member adding their own unique flavor to our dynamic. I am the youngest of six siblings, which includes five remarkable sisters and one exceptionally influential brother. Growing up in such a large family meant that every day was filled with a symphony of personalities and experiences, each contributing to the rich tapestry of our shared history. My brother, being the only other male in the family, held a particularly special place in my life. His presence was a guiding force, shaping much of my understanding of the world and providing a sense of security and camaraderie that only a sibling can offer. Let me dive deeper into the lives of my siblings, focusing especially on my brother, whose impact on my journey has been both profound and enduring.

My brother was the quintessential comedian of our family, the one who effortlessly balanced the roles of protector and entertainer amidst the sea of sisters who outnumbered him. With an innate sense of humor and a quick wit, he had an extraordinary ability to lift our spirits, no matter how grim the situation seemed. His jokes and playful antics were a constant source of joy, transforming even the most challenging moments into opportunities for laughter and connection. Beyond his role as the family jester, he often stepped into a quasi-fatherly role, offering guidance and wisdom that belied his years. Whether it was through a well-timed quip or heartfelt advice, he had a unique talent for brightening our days and providing a steady source.

However, life took a devastating turn for him. My brother faced a long and harrowing struggle with drug addiction, a battle that relentlessly eroded his vitality and hope. Over the years, his dependency grew worse, dragging him further into a cycle of despair and helplessness. When I received the news of his overdose, the shock was immediate and paralyzing. It was a visceral blow that rendered me motionless, as if the earth had shifted beneath my feet. The details of that day remain etched in my mind: the frantic phone call, the disbelief, and the overwhelming surge of grief. His passing left an irreplaceable void in my life, a deep and aching absence that words struggle to capture. The pain of losing him was immense, a crushing weight that pressed down on my chest. But this loss was only the precursor to a cascade of subsequent heartaches and struggles that followed, each one compounding the sorrow of his absence.

In the early 2000s, our family faced a heart-wrenching tragedy when my sister took her own life. The impact of this loss was profoundly devastating, unraveling the very fabric of our lives. Her passing was not just a loss but a seismic shift that left a void too immense to measure. I had always prided myself on my resilience, believing that no matter what challenges life threw at me, I would find a way to endure and overcome. Yet, the enormity of this grief was unlike anything I had ever encountered. It was an all-consuming sorrow that went beyond mere sadness; it was a raw, deep-seated pain that permeated every aspect of my being. This pain was not just emotional but physical, a visceral ache that felt like it was tearing me apart from the inside out. The sense of helplessness and the unrelenting weight of the loss seemed to press down on me, leaving me grappling with an intensity of grief I had never imagined possible.

The grief of losing my brother and sister was a crushing weight, an all-consuming force that seemed to envelop every aspect of my existence. It felt as though I was caught in the eye of a relentless storm, with torrential winds and unending rain battering me from all directions, leaving me disoriented and helpless. Their absence was a gaping void in my life, a stark reminder of the fragility of our connections. I had to grapple with the harsh reality that their laughter, their presence, and the shared moments of joy were irrevocably gone. The world outside continued to spin with indifferent efficiency, advancing relentlessly like a clock whose hands never paused. Each passing second was a stark reminder that life marches on, indifferent to the personal tragedies we endure. I was forced to navigate this unyielding current of time, struggling to find my footing while the emotional toll left me feeling hollow and drained. The pain of their loss was a constant shadow, haunting every step I took as I endeavored to keep moving forward, even when every part of me longed for a moment of reprieve.

Amidst this intense personal turmoil, I came to understand the vital importance of finding effective coping mechanisms and the need to keep moving forward. Grief, as I discovered, is far from a linear process; rather, it unfolds in a chaotic and unpredictable manner. There were days when the weight of my sorrow felt almost unbearable, leaving me feeling as though I might crumble under the pressure. On such days, every task seemed monumental, and the prospect of continuing seemed out of reach. However, there were also moments of surprising resilience, when I managed to muster the strength to place one foot in front of the other. This determination was often driven by a profound sense of duty and a responsibility to those who depended on me. Equally important was the unwavering support I received from those around me—friends, family, and even colleagues—whose empathy and encouragement provided a lifeline during my darkest hours. Their presence offered a semblance of normalcy and hope, which played a crucial role in helping me navigate through the tumultuous waves of grief.

During this period, my work became an unexpected sanctuary amidst the turmoil. I immersed myself in my tasks with an almost obsessive fervor, hoping that the routine and structure of my job would provide a distraction from the overwhelming emotions I was grappling with. The demands of my professional life, while demanding, offered a semblance of normalcy and a temporary escape from the crushing weight of my grief. However, despite my best efforts to remain anchored in work, there were moments when the intensity of the pain became unbearable. On these occasions, I found myself needing to step away, allowing myself the necessary time to focus on my mental well-being. This was a sobering realization—a recognition that while work provided temporary relief, it was not a substitute for addressing the deep-seated sorrow I was experiencing. I had to confront my grief head-on, allowing myself the space to truly feel the loss, process my emotions, and begin the slow and challenging journey of healing.

In the midst of all this turmoil and uncertainty, I sought solace in my faith, which became a crucial anchor during these turbulent times. As I faced the darkness and challenges, I found myself turning to prayer and reflection more frequently. It was during these intense periods of struggle that my connection with God deepened profoundly. I immersed myself in spiritual practices, drawing strength from sacred texts and religious rituals that had always been a part of my life but now took on a new significance.

My faith evolved into a cornerstone of resilience, providing me with a sense of purpose and direction amid the overwhelming pain. Each day, I grappled with the emotional weight of my circumstances, yet my belief that everything unfolds according to a divine plan offered me a glimmer of hope. I embraced the notion that there is a greater design at play, one that transcends my immediate suffering. This conviction became a source of comfort, assuring me that, although the trials were intense and seemingly unending, they were part of a larger narrative. With time, I held onto the assurance that the sharp edges of pain would eventually soften, and that through this journey, I would find healing and understanding.

During this period, I was grappling with a series of personal health challenges that compounded the already overwhelming stress I was experiencing. My blood pressure became erratic, fluctuating unpredictably and adding to my physical discomfort. This instability not only made me feel unwell but also intensified the emotional strain I was under as I struggled to manage my grief and balance my work responsibilities. The constant need to monitor my blood pressure, adhere to a strict diet, and manage medication added another layer of complexity to my daily routine. Despite these difficulties, I remained resolute. I understood that, much like the unceasing motion of a clock on the wall, life continued to move forward regardless of my personal struggles. This realization drove me to persevere, reminding me that I had to keep pushing through each day, even when it felt nearly impossible. There are more important things in life than hate and judgment; life is too short to focus on negativity.

    I want to express my profound gratitude to everyone who stood by me through these challenging trials. My friends, family, and church members were an immeasurable source of support and comfort during this difficult period. Their unwavering presence and heartfelt kindness served as a vital cushion against the harsh realities of my loss. Each thoughtful gesture, whether it was a reassuring word, a helping hand, or simply their presence, played a crucial role in alleviating the weight of my grief. Their steadfast support provided me with the strength and solace I desperately needed when I felt most vulnerable. I am deeply thankful for their compassion, which not only eased my burden but also reminded me of the enduring power of human connection and the importance of having a supportive community in times of sorrow.

    Reflecting on this period, it becomes clear how crucial a strong support system is when facing grief and adversity. A support system can encompass a variety of resources— friends who listen and empathize, family members who provide unwavering encouragement, or support groups where shared experiences create a sense of belonging and mutual understanding. The presence of such a network can profoundly impact your ability to cope with loss or hardship, offering both emotional and practical support.

When grappling with grief, it's vital to remember that you don't have to navigate these turbulent times in isolation. Reaching out to others can be a lifeline, providing not just companionship but also diverse perspectives and advice that can help lighten the emotional load. Engaging with those who offer comfort, whether through personal conversations, professional counseling, or communal support settings, can make a substantial difference. By allowing others to support you, you acknowledge the value of human connection and create opportunities for healing and resilience.

Everything unfolds according to a larger plan, even if the reasons remain hidden from us in the moment. Grieving is a deeply personal journey that varies for each individual, and it's perfectly okay to navigate it gradually, at your own pace. Embrace each small step as part of the healing process, understanding that it's natural to experience a range of emotions and setbacks along the way. With consistent support from loved ones and the passage of time, healing becomes a real possibility. Just as the clock on the wall continuously ticks forward, marking the passage of each moment, so too does time advance, bringing with it the potential for renewed hope and brighter days.

Each day offers a new opportunity for growth and recovery, and as time progresses, it gently guides us toward a future where the pain of today can transform into the promise of a more hopeful tomorrow.

Chapter 5
Destiny and Determination

At twenty-four years old, juggling the responsibilities of raising two young children, I found myself at a profound crossroads, gazing uncertainly at a future I had yet to fully grasp or envision. My life's journey, marked by its unorthodox nature, had been a tapestry woven with the threads of five marriages, each one leaving its own indelible mark on my heart and mind. Alongside these personal transformations, I navigated through a series of career shifts, each one offering unique challenges and opportunities that tested and refined my abilities. My experiences ranged from brief stints in various professions to more significant, yet often transient, roles that shaped my professional identity.

Amidst the shifting sands of my personal and professional life, I encountered a myriad of experiences that, while sometimes tumultuous, contributed richly to my growth. Looking back, I see that each marriage, every career change, and each life experience—whether it was a triumph or a setback—played a crucial role in sculpting my current self. These moments, though often challenging and unpredictable, were instrumental in shaping my understanding of who I am and what I seek in life. They provided invaluable lessons that contributed to my evolving sense of self and purpose. Despite the turbulence and the unforeseen paths that life has presented, I can reflect on this journey with a deep sense of acceptance and clarity, recognizing that every step, both forward and backward, has been integral to my personal development and self-discovery.

I have always harbored a firm conviction that fate should not be the sole determinant of my life's direction. My guiding principle has been to remain steadfast in my true self and to hold fast to my faith, regardless of the external circumstances or the challenges that may arise. It is this unwavering adherence to my core values that has shaped my journey and led me to the place where I stand today.

Reflecting on my life, I can see that my marriage has been a cornerstone of my existence—a significant facet of what seems to be my destined path. Through the trials and triumphs, our bond has been a source of strength and stability. My continued commitment to this union is a testament to the deep connection we share and the belief that our relationship is integral to my journey.

I am profoundly grateful for the guidance and support that I have received along the way. My faith has been a beacon, illuminating the path through both serene and tumultuous times. In moments of uncertainty, I have found solace in my trust that a higher power is steering me towards a purpose greater than I could have envisioned on my own.

Thank you, God, for your unwavering guidance and for orchestrating the events that have led me to this place of contentment and fulfillment. Your presence in my life has been a source of profound reassurance and hope, shaping my experiences and helping me navigate the complexities of life with grace and resilience.

Reflecting on my past, I can't help but feel a pang of regret about some of the choices I made, particularly when it comes to selecting the father of my children. With the benefit of hindsight and the wisdom I've accumulated over the years, it's clear that my decisions could have been more thoughtful and deliberate. I often think about how different my life might have been if I had approached those crucial decisions with the knowledge I have now.

The phrase "youth is wasted on the young" rings true for me. When I was younger, I believed I had all the answers and a firm grasp on what was best for my future. I was confident in my choices, convinced that my instincts and desires would lead me to the right path. Yet, as time passed, I came to understand that youth often blinds us to the complexities and consequences of our actions. It's a bittersweet realization: I thought I knew everything, but in reality, I knew very little.

The saying "Been there, done that" perfectly encapsulates my journey. I've lived through the lessons that only experience can teach. And now, I find myself sharing this mantra with others, especially the younger generation. I urge them to embrace life's experiences and learn from them, for it is through these trials and triumphs that we gain the most valuable insights. Each experience, whether good or bad, is a teacher, shaping us into more understanding and wiser individuals. Keep living, keep learning, and remember that life's most profound lessons often come from the paths we take and the choices we make along the way.

DON'T HATE

Life has exposed me to the harsh realities of the world, often through the lens of violence and tragedy. One of the most vivid and unsettling memories I have involves a series of incidents with firearms that left an indelible mark on my psyche. I recall with unsettling clarity an incident that occurred in my mother's house, where the atmosphere was abruptly shattered by a violent confrontation. My two older sisters' boyfriends, who were both heavily involved in a heated argument, escalated their altercation to a devastating degree. In a moment of sheer chaos, one of them pulled out a gun and fired it at the other. The deafening sound of the gunshot was followed by an eerie silence as the gravity of the situation set in.

Caught in the midst of this traumatic event, I felt paralyzed by fear and confusion. The urgency of the moment made me realize the precariousness of my own safety, and I faced a critical decision. With the immediate threat of police involvement looming, I decided to leave the scene with the boyfriend who had fired the shot, hoping to distance myself from the turmoil and evade any further complications. The decision was driven by a desperate need to escape the chaos, rather than a clear sense of right or wrong.

Fortunately, the man who had been shot survived the ordeal, but the experience was nothing short of harrowing. It left me grappling with the raw, unsettling reality of violence and its impact on those caught in its wake. The memory of that night continues to haunt me, serving as a stark reminder of the fragility of life and the unforeseen dangers that can arise from human conflict.

DON'T HATE

Another profoundly traumatic incident occurred at my aunt's house, where a young boy, driven by a reckless impulse, decided to engage in the dangerous game of Russian roulette. In a tragic twist of fate, the revolver he was handling discharged a bullet directly into his head. The atmosphere was charged with panic and disbelief as the boy fell to the ground, blood pooling around him. Against all odds, he survived the harrowing ordeal, though the extent of his injuries was severe and the psychological scars deep. This shocking event served as a jarring reminder of life's inherent unpredictability and the perilous outcomes of impulsive behavior. The gravity of the situation underscored the fragile nature of existence and the precarious balance between life and death, leaving a lasting impact on everyone who witnessed or heard about it.

One particularly harrowing experience occurred when I was living in Pittsburgh, Atlanta, and was robbed at gunpoint in my own home. The neighborhood where I resided had a reputation for being particularly rough, with crime being a common occurrence. On that terrifying night, I was startled awake by the sound of someone breaking into my house. The intruder, brandishing a gun and demanding valuables, created an atmosphere of sheer panic and helplessness. The sense of violation and fear I felt in that moment was profound and left a lasting impact on my perception of safety and security. This traumatic event significantly influenced my stance on gun laws and regulations. It became glaringly apparent to me that stricter gun control measures are crucial. The prevalence of firearms in situations like these often escalates conflicts rather than resolving them, contributing to a cycle of violence that could be mitigated by more stringent regulations.

Through these trials, I have cultivated a deep sense of resilience and determination that has become integral to my approach to life. Each challenge, whether personal or professional, has fortified my ability to persevere and face adversity with unwavering strength. My journey through marriage has profoundly shaped my understanding of true unity and commitment. The shared experiences, trials, and triumphs with my partner have underscored the importance of mutual support and unwavering dedication. I have come to firmly believe that a relationship extends beyond mere cohabitation; it must be rooted in the sacred institution of marriage, which I view as a profound commitment and partnership. This conviction is not just a principle but a guiding force in my life, influencing my decisions and shaping my approach to relationships. For me, the institution of marriage represents a foundation of trust, respect, and shared values that transcends the superficial aspects of a relationship, and it has been this belief that has consistently steered me in making choices that align with my core values and long-term vision.

My first marriage, which I entered into during my teenage years, was with the father of my children and lasted until I was twenty-five. This early relationship, fraught with its own set of challenges and growth opportunities, was pivotal in shaping my understanding of what partnership and commitment truly mean. Navigating the complexities of young adulthood while building a life with someone and raising children together taught me invaluable lessons about dedication, compromise, and the depth of emotional connection required to sustain a lasting relationship.

In the years following, my subsequent marriages varied significantly in both length and character, each one adding a unique layer to my perspective on the institution of marriage. While these relationships had their own distinct dynamics and outcomes, they collectively reinforced my belief in the sanctity of marriage as a profound and enduring commitment. Each union, regardless of its duration or eventual outcome, contributed to a deeper appreciation for the seriousness of entering into a lifelong partnership.

I approach relationships with a sense of gravitas and intentionality. My decision to be with someone is never taken lightly; it is driven by a genuine belief in the potential for a lifelong, meaningful union. I understand that a true partnership requires more than just emotional investment — it demands a shared vision for the future, mutual respect, and unwavering dedication.

Throughout my career, I've explored a range of job opportunities, each contributing to my professional development in unique ways. However, I have come to a clear realization: I thrive most in environments where I have autonomy and control over my work. My tenure at MCI stands out as a particularly rewarding chapter. During that time, I not only had the opportunity to contribute meaningfully to the company's objectives but also succeeded in creating a stable and prosperous future for my children. This experience underscored the importance of aligning one's career path with personal goals and values. It became evident that self-employment or roles that offer substantial independence often yield the highest levels of satisfaction and fulfillment. This understanding has guided my career choices, reinforcing my belief that the greatest personal and professional rewards come from carving out one's own path and being in charge of one's destiny.

When entering a relationship or partnership, it's essential to take time to ensure that your expectations and long-term goals align with those of your partner. This alignment is crucial because differing expectations can lead to misunderstandings and conflicts over time. Compatibility goes beyond mere personal interests and hobbies; it involves a deeper understanding of each other's life aspirations, values, and priorities.

Effective communication plays a vital role in this process. Open, honest dialogue about your individual goals, whether they pertain to career ambitions, family plans, or personal growth, is key to fostering mutual understanding. It's important to discuss these aspects early on and revisit them periodically as your relationship evolves.

Furthermore, valuing and respecting each other's perspectives and ambitions contributes significantly to a more fulfilling partnership. Taking the time to listen to your partner's viewpoints and showing empathy towards their aspirations helps build a strong foundation of trust and support. This approach not only aids in resolving conflicts but also enhances the overall quality of the relationship, as both partners feel heard and appreciated. By nurturing these elements, you create a dynamic where both individuals can grow together harmoniously and achieve shared goals while respecting each other's individual dreams.

Reflecting on the issue of gun violence, my personal experiences have profoundly shaped my conviction that substantial reform is necessary. While the fundamental right to self-defense is a principle I acknowledge and respect, it has become evident through my observations that not every individual should have unrestricted access to firearms. The alarming incidents I have witnessed — ranging from local tragedies to high-profile violent events — highlight the urgent need for more rigorous gun control measures. The pervasive nature of gun violence inflicts deep and lasting damage on communities, tearing apart the fabric of social cohesion and instilling fear among residents. This violence not only results in immediate harm but also contributes to long-term psychological and social consequences. In light of these observations, it is imperative that we advocate for comprehensive changes in gun legislation aimed at safeguarding individuals and mitigating the frequency and severity of such tragic events. By pursuing more effective regulations, we can work towards a future where communities are better protected and the incidence of violence is significantly reduced.

Despite the challenges and roughness of the neighborhoods I've called home in Atlanta, I have learned to navigate these environments with a profound sense of faith and respect. The gritty realities of urban life have tested my resilience and character, but they have also reinforced my belief in the transformative power of mutual respect and understanding. I approach every interaction with the principle that I should value others as I wish to be valued myself. This reciprocal approach has become a guiding force in my life, helping me bridge divides that might otherwise seem insurmountable.

Reflecting on my journey through five marriages, countless job changes, and several intense, sometimes harrowing experiences, I recognize the deep lessons I have learned about destiny, determination, and self-awareness. Each relationship and job has shaped me, teaching me about love, endurance, and the importance of knowing oneself. Through the highs and lows, I have developed a nuanced understanding of my own path and the broader contours of my life's narrative.

I harbor no regrets; instead, I hold a profound sense of gratitude for the varied experiences that have defined my journey. Each step along the way—whether marked by struggle or success—has contributed to my personal growth and deepened my understanding of my place in the world. As I continue to forge ahead, I remain committed to embracing growth, nurturing resilience, and maintaining a steadfast faith in the journey of life.

Chapter 6
Understanding and Venting

Life is a rich and intricate tapestry, intricately woven from the diverse threads of our individual experiences, deeply-held beliefs, and the often-overwhelming societal pressures that influence our daily lives. As we look at the contemporary world, it becomes abundantly clear that certain issues, such as gun control and women's rights, persistently dominate the societal landscape and provoke vigorous debates. These issues are not just abstract concepts or distant concerns; they are deeply entwined with the personal narratives and lived experiences of countless individuals.

To truly grasp these complex matters, it is essential to examine them not only through a broad and general perspective but also through the intimate and personal lenses that shape our understanding. This chapter aims to unravel these intricate issues by intertwining my own personal journey and the lessons I have gleaned through my experiences. Rather than presenting a mere exposition of my viewpoints, this chapter serves as a reflective exploration of the multifaceted challenges we encounter. It is an invitation to acknowledge and confront these pressing issues with both resilience and empathy, recognizing their profound impact on our collective human experience and the urgent need for continued dialogue and understanding.

Gun Control: A Call for Fairness

Growing up in an era where discussions about gun control dominate national conversations, I have seen firsthand the profound effects that inadequate regulation can have on communities. My perspective on firearms has been shaped by a combination of limited personal exposure and the sobering images and stories relayed through media coverage of gun-related incidents. These experiences have cemented my belief in the critical need for well-considered and effective gun laws.

To me, gun control is not about imposing unnecessary restrictions but about ensuring that those who choose to possess firearms are subject to thorough vetting processes and comprehensive training. The goal is to create a balanced framework that upholds the rights of responsible gun owners while simultaneously enhancing public safety. In an ideal world, gun laws would be embraced as essential safeguards rather than contentious issues. They would serve as proactive measures to prevent tragedies and protect individuals from the potential misuse of firearms.

The current environment, where the sheer availability of guns can seem overwhelming, underscores the need for a more regulated approach. The push for fair gun control is driven by a desire to implement sensible and practical measures that prevent harm and ensure that firearms are not accessible to those who might misuse them. This approach recognizes the complexity of the issue and seeks to address it in a way that respects individual rights while prioritizing the well-being and safety of the broader community.

Women's Rights: Respect and Autonomy

Women's rights represent a critical intersection where personal experiences meet societal expectations. Despite decades of progress, the journey toward gender equality remains fraught with challenges, and the autonomy of women is often disregarded. It is profoundly disheartening to witness how entrenched societal norms and external pressures continue to shape and sometimes undermine women's rights.

The belief that women's rights can be defined or restricted by others reflects a fundamental misunderstanding of autonomy and individuality. Every woman, like every individual, deserves to have her rights and needs addressed based on her own choices and unique circumstances, rather than being shaped by external judgments or societal constraints. Women's rights should be grounded in a framework of respect and empathy, ensuring that their voices are not only heard but valued in all areas of life.

This approach calls for a shift from viewing women's rights as merely a series of legal entitlements to understanding them as a profound quest for respect, dignity, and personal recognition. It involves acknowledging that each woman's experiences and needs are distinct and should be approached with a deep sense of understanding. Gender equality is not just a matter of policy; it is a moral imperative that demands ongoing vigilance and a commitment to fostering an environment where every woman can fully exercise her rights and autonomy.

Personal Struggles and Overcoming Adversity

Reflecting on my life, I have endured substantial health challenges, particularly due to lupus, a chronic autoimmune disease that has significantly impacted my daily existence. From an early age, managing the unpredictable symptoms of lupus—ranging from joint pain and fatigue to skin rashes and organ inflammation—required me to depend heavily on my family's unwavering support. My parents, siblings, and extended family members provided not only physical assistance but also emotional encouragement, which proved indispensable during periods of intense suffering and uncertainty.

This ongoing battle with illness has been a profound teacher, instilling in me the importance of resilience. Each flare-up or setback underscored the necessity of navigating life's adversities with a combination of determination and faith. I learned that resilience is not merely about enduring hardship but about facing each challenge with a proactive mindset and an unyielding spirit.

The difficulties I faced were not just physical but emotional and psychological as well. They tested my resolve and highlighted the significance of maintaining a sense of purpose and focus on my personal goals. Despite the considerable pain and frequent obstacles, I found strength in my support network and the grace of God. This divine grace, coupled with the steadfast support of my family, played a crucial role in helping me persevere through each trial.

As I moved through these health challenges, I discovered invaluable lessons about the necessity of managing one's health proactively, setting and pursuing personal goals with unwavering commitment, and resisting the temptation to let adversity derail my aspirations. My experience has not only shaped my understanding of personal strength but also reaffirmed the importance of holding onto hope and continually striving toward my goals, regardless of the obstacles that may arise.

Dealing with Criticism and Jealousy

In any journey toward achieving success, encountering criticism and jealousy is almost inevitable. These reactions often emerge from a place of deep-seated insecurity or a compulsion to undermine others in order to feel superior. When people criticize or express envy towards your achievements, it is frequently an attempt to diminish your accomplishments to elevate their own sense of self-worth. Recognizing this underlying motive is crucial, as it allows you to remain steadfast and focused on your own path, despite the distractions.

Criticism, in its many forms, can sometimes be constructive and offer valuable feedback. However, when criticism is rooted in jealousy or malicious intent, it becomes essential to rise above it and not let it derail your progress. People who harbor negative feelings often do so because of their own personal insecurities or failures. Understanding that these individuals may be struggling with their own challenges can help you manage such situations with grace and composure.

Instead of allowing negative comments to deter you, view them as an opportunity to reinforce your commitment to your goals. Use the energy that could be spent on frustration or self-doubt to fuel your determination and drive. By maintaining a positive mindset and focusing on personal growth, you can navigate through these challenges more effectively. Remember, everyone has the potential to realize their dreams; the difference lies in how tenaciously one pursues them and the resilience with which one faces obstacles.

When faced with jealousy or criticism, it's often a reflection of the critic's own struggles and limitations rather than a true assessment of your achievements. By concentrating on your path and embracing a forward-looking perspective, you can transform potential setbacks into stepping stones towards your success. Maintaining this focus will enable you to rise above the negativity and continue to make meaningful progress towards your goals.

Embracing Empathy and Love

Despite the inevitable waves of negativity and criticism that may come your way throughout life, it is imperative to approach each situation with a mindset rooted in empathy and love. The human tendency to hold onto resentment or harbor anger towards those who criticize can be not only emotionally draining but also counterproductive to your personal growth. Instead of succumbing to these negative emotions, which can cloud your judgment and hinder your progress, focus on elevating both yourself and those around you by nurturing a spirit of compassion and understanding.

The world, with its myriad of opinions and judgments, can often present a challenging landscape. From societal pressures to personal criticisms, these external forces can sometimes feel overwhelming. However, the most effective antidote to such negativity is to embody kindness and love in all your interactions. Support others in their pursuits, genuinely celebrate their achievements, and maintain a positive attitude even in the face of adversity. By choosing to act with kindness, you not only enrich your own life but also foster a more supportive and encouraging environment for everyone around you. This collective positive energy can lead to more meaningful connections and a sense of community that thrives on mutual respect and empathy.

In summary, navigating the complexities of societal issues such as gun control and women's rights demands more than a superficial understanding; it requires a deep, nuanced comprehension of the historical, cultural, and political factors at play, coupled with a steadfast commitment to fairness and respect for differing perspectives. Addressing these issues effectively involves critically examining the diverse viewpoints and experiences that shape public discourse, while striving to find common ground and advocate for policies that promote justice and equality.

Personal experiences, whether grappling with health challenges or enduring criticism, provide profound lessons in resilience and perseverance. Each obstacle encountered offers a unique opportunity for personal growth and development.

Facing these trials with a sense of determination and fortitude can transform adversity into a source of strength and insight. By maintaining a clear focus on your goals, embracing a spirit of empathy towards others, and rising above negativity, you can navigate these challenges effectively and make meaningful contributions to the world around you.

It is essential to express your frustrations and voice your opinions, but always strive to do so with an understanding of and respect for the perspectives of others. Recognize that every challenge you face is not merely a hurdle but a stepping stone toward growth, and every criticism encountered is a chance to demonstrate your inner strength and resolve. By continuously striving to elevate both yourself and those around you, you foster an environment where true success is measured not only by achieving personal goals but also by the ability to remain authentic to oneself while nurturing a spirit of compassion and love for others.

Chapter 7
Encountering the Unexpected

Life has a remarkable way of guiding us onto unexpected paths, often leading us through detours that unveil the most profound and transformative discoveries. My journey began with the initial steps of college, where I had envisioned a straightforward trajectory towards a conventional career. However, life had other plans. Instead of following a linear path, I found myself immersed in the exhilarating challenge of running a successful business. This phase was marked by countless late nights, strategic decisions, and the thrill of entrepreneurial victories, as well as the inevitable setbacks that come with building something from the ground up.

Navigating through this whirlwind of business responsibilities was accompanied by a series of personal challenges that tested my resilience and adaptability. From balancing work with personal relationships to overcoming unexpected crises, each obstacle became a catalyst for personal growth and self-discovery. These experiences enriched my understanding of perseverance and taught me valuable lessons about managing adversity with grace.

As time went on, the dynamic nature of my career and personal life led me to a pivotal moment of introspection. Driven by a newfound passion and a desire for further professional development, I made the bold decision to return to school with a focus on marketing. This choice was not just about acquiring new skills but was also a reflection of my evolving aspirations and the pursuit of a more fulfilling path.

The culmination of this journey was a profound encounter — one that significantly altered the course of my life. This encounter, whether it was a mentorship, a critical turning point, or an epiphany, served as a catalyst for change and reinforced the unpredictability of life's journey. My story is not merely one of career evolution but a testament to the resilience and growth that arise from embracing life's unpredictable nature and the transformative experiences it brings.

I embarked on my academic journey with grand ambitions, enrolling in college with the intention of securing a degree in Business Administration. Fueled by a strong desire to immerse myself in the complexities of the business world, I envisioned a future where I would manage and lead within the corporate sector, contributing to strategic decision-making and organizational growth. My initial coursework was deeply engaging, and I relished every opportunity to explore topics such as finance, marketing, and management.

However, as my college years progressed, an unexpected shift occurred. I found myself increasingly captivated by a field that diverged sharply from my original path: dentistry. This newfound interest led me to explore certification as a dental assistant. The decision to pivot from business to dentistry was not made lightly; it was a profound change that required re-evaluating my career goals and aspirations.

DON'T HATE

The journey into the dental field proved to be both challenging and enriching. As a dental assistant, I acquired a distinctive set of skills, including patient care techniques, dental procedures, and the nuances of working within a clinical environment. I developed a deeper appreciation for the intricate nature of dental health and the importance of compassionate patient interactions. This hands-on experience offered me a fresh perspective on the healthcare sector, which was both fulfilling and intellectually stimulating.

Balancing the demands of working in dentistry while maintaining my business studies was a formidable task. It required meticulous time management and adaptability. Nonetheless, this dual focus enriched my professional capabilities, allowing me to integrate the analytical and strategic skills from my business education with the practical and empathetic aspects of dental care. This diverse skill set not only broadened my professional horizons but also prepared me to navigate a range of challenges and opportunities in various facets of my life.

Armed with a robust background in Business Administration and a specialized certification in dental assistance, I embarked on a new professional journey with a surge of confidence and determination. My dual expertise equipped me with a unique blend of business acumen and hands-on service skills, which I leveraged to make a significant impact in the business world

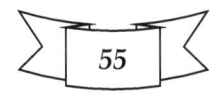

I was entrusted with a pivotal role, managing three distinct stores simultaneously. This responsibility encompassed a broad range of tasks and challenges, requiring a multifaceted approach. My role involved overseeing various critical aspects of the business, including human resources management and customer service training. Each store presented its own set of challenges and opportunities, and my goal was to ensure a seamless and efficient operation across all locations.

In the realm of human resources, I was tasked with recruiting, training, and developing a diverse team of employees. This aspect of my role was particularly demanding, as it required not only an understanding of business principles but also a deep sense of empathy and strategic foresight. I implemented training programs designed to elevate staff performance and foster a positive work environment. By focusing on clear communication, I ensured that team members were aligned with the company's values and objectives, which significantly contributed to overall productivity and morale.

Customer service training was another crucial component of my responsibilities. Drawing from my background in dental assistance, where patient care and interpersonal skills are paramount, I emphasized the importance of delivering exceptional service. I developed comprehensive training modules that addressed various customer interaction scenarios, helping staff refine their skills in handling inquiries, resolving complaints, and creating a welcoming atmosphere for customers. This hands-on approach not only improved service standards but also enhanced customer satisfaction and loyalty.

The role demanded a high level of adaptability and proactivity, traits that were cultivated through my previous experiences. In business administration, I had learned the importance of strategic planning and resource management. In dental assistance, I had honed my ability to handle complex situations with calm and precision. These skills were invaluable as I navigated the complexities of managing a large team and addressing the multifaceted needs of the stores.

Overall, managing three stores was a transformative experience that reinforced my understanding of effective communication, the value of empathy in leadership, and the necessity of strategic thinking. These lessons have become foundational elements of my professional approach, enabling me to handle future challenges with a well-rounded perspective and a commitment to excellence.

Despite achieving significant success in the business world, I felt an unfulfilled urge to deepen my expertise and broaden my skill set. Managing my bookstore had illuminated a critical gap in my knowledge: a comprehensive understanding of marketing. This realization was prompted by the challenges I faced in promoting my store effectively and the increasing competition within the retail industry. My initial strategies, while somewhat effective, seemed insufficient in the evolving market landscape.

Recognizing this gap as a significant barrier to further growth, I made the pivotal decision to return to school with a focus on Marketing. This choice was not merely about enhancing my promotional tactics but was driven by a deeper ambition to grasp the complexities of market dynamics. I wanted to delve into the intricacies of market trends, analyze consumer behavior patterns, and master the art of crafting compelling promotional strategies. My goal was to develop a nuanced understanding that would enable me to connect more effectively with potential customers and expand my business's reach.

Enrolling in a marketing program provided me with a structured framework to explore these areas in-depth. I engaged with coursework that covered everything from consumer psychology and market research to digital marketing and branding strategies. This academic journey was complemented by practical projects and case studies, which allowed me to apply theoretical concepts to real-world scenarios.

The knowledge and skills I acquired through this new academic endeavor proved invaluable. I was able to refine my business approach, implementing sophisticated marketing strategies that resonated with a broader audience. This not only enhanced my ability to promote my bookstore more effectively but also significantly improved customer engagement and satisfaction. The insights gained from studying marketing transformed my business operations, enabling me to better meet the needs of my customers and adapt to an ever-changing market.

During this pivotal year as I was pursuing my marketing degree, I encountered an individual who would unexpectedly become a central figure in my life. This person, whom I later detailed in my book How I Fell in Love with My

Stalker, entered my world in a manner that was both surprising and unsettling.

Our relationship commenced in a rather unconventional fashion, marked by persistent and increasingly intrusive behaviors that soon became deeply troubling. What started as seemingly benign interactions quickly escalated into a pattern of obsessive and alarming conduct. The intensity of these behaviors thrust me into a state of constant anxiety and fear, forcing me to confront a series of psychological and emotional challenges that I had never before encountered.

The experience was profoundly disorienting and compelled me to reevaluate my own sense of security and self-worth. I had to navigate a complex emotional landscape, grappling with the invasive nature of this person's attention and the unsettling realization of my own vulnerability. It was through this tumultuous period that I gained profound insights into the importance of intuition, the necessity of maintaining personal boundaries, and the resilience required to withstand such an intense situation.

The ordeal with my stalker became a significant turning point, reshaping my approach to various facets of my personal and professional life. It instilled in me a heightened awareness of the subtle warning signs in relationships and situations, reinforcing the importance of trusting my instincts. Additionally, this harrowing experience ignited a creative spark within me, driving me to channel my emotions and the lessons I had learned into my writing. The result was the creation of my debut book, which emerged as a therapeutic outlet and a means to process and share the profound impact of that period in my life.

Reflecting on my journey, I realize that the unexpected twists and turns were not merely obstacles but profound opportunities for growth and self-discovery. Each experience, from my early career shifts to the daunting challenges of dealing with a stalker, played a pivotal role in shaping the person I am today.

My career began with a degree in Business Administration, which provided a solid foundation in strategic thinking, financial management, and organizational skills. I anticipated a conventional career path within the corporate world. However, life had other plans. I ventured into dental assistance, a field far removed from my initial academic focus. This shift was driven by a desire to explore different aspects of professional life and contribute meaningfully to others' well-being. The hands-on experience in dental assistance taught me invaluable lessons in patient care, attention to detail, and empathy—skills that proved crucial in various facets of my life.

In parallel, I dabbled in marketing, where I applied my business acumen to create compelling campaigns and drive engagement. This experience honed my creativity and adaptability, allowing me to understand market dynamics and consumer behavior. The blend of these diverse roles—dental assistance, marketing, and business administration—endowed me with a versatile skill set that proved to be a great asset.

Amid these professional endeavors, an unexpected and unsettling encounter with a stalker introduced a new dimension of challenge. The situation was profoundly distressing and forced me to confront my vulnerabilities. Navigating through this period was one of the most challenging phases of my life. It was a test of not only my personal safety but also my mental resilience and emotional fortitude.

The ordeal with the stalker was not just about managing fear but also about understanding the importance of listening to my instincts and setting boundaries. I had to learn to navigate the complexities of legal and personal safety while maintaining my composure and focus. This experience reinforced the necessity of self-preservation and taught me the importance of trusting my intuition in protecting my well-being.

Despite the difficulties, these experiences collectively fostered a profound sense of resilience and self-awareness. They taught me that adversity, while uncomfortable and challenging, often provides the greatest opportunities for personal development. The skills and insights gained from dealing with such unexpected situations have become integral to my approach to life and work.

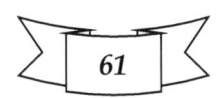

As I continue with my writing and professional endeavors, I carry with me the lessons learned from these diverse experiences. They remind me that while life is inherently unpredictable, it is through navigating these unexpected moments that we often uncover our true strength and purpose. Each challenge and detour has contributed to my growth, reinforcing my belief that every experience, no matter how daunting, has the potential to shape and define our path.

In embracing these lessons, I approach each new chapter of my life with a greater sense of confidence and clarity. The journey has taught me that resilience is not just about enduring hardships but about transforming them into stepping stones towards greater understanding and fulfillment.

Chapter 8
Growing Up and Moving On

My transition into adulthood began in 1990 when I was nearing 15, a time when many teenagers are exploring their identities and future paths. This period marked a significant turning point in my life, as I met the father of my children, a connection that would profoundly shape my future. Driven by a strong desire for independence and a place to belong, I encountered a man who offered the stability and security I was seeking. Our relationship was unconventional and not in line with societal norms, but it became a crucial source of growth and learning for me. We had a mutual understanding: I needed a home, and he was willing to provide it. This arrangement, though unexpected, was instrumental in my personal development, helping me discover my own strength and resilience. So, while it may be easy to judge from the outside, I encourage you to look beyond the surface and appreciate the complexities of my journey.

Living with someone at such a young age introduced me to adult responsibilities far earlier than most of my peers. I suddenly found myself managing household chores, budgeting, and making decisions that were typically reserved for those much older. This experience was both challenging and enlightening; it forced me to mature quickly and confront realities that many teenagers don't encounter until much later in life. Navigating the complexities of a relationship that felt advanced for my years was no small feat. I had to balance the natural inclinations of a young person to explore and seek new experiences with the demands of a more settled, domestic life. This period of my life was marked by an intense inner struggle between my youthful desire for freedom and exploration and the reality of the responsibilities I had taken on.

The relationship itself was a mixed blessing; on one hand, it provided me with a sense of stability and security that was comforting amidst the chaos of my circumstances. On the other hand, it also imposed certain limitations on my freedom, as I was often bound by the expectations and commitments that came with being in a serious relationship. The significant age difference between us added another layer of complexity, influencing the power dynamics and the way we communicated and interacted with each other. While my partner had more life experience and often took on a guiding role, I sometimes felt overshadowed and struggled to assert my own identity and desires.

I was still in the process of discovering who I was and what I wanted from life, and there were moments when I felt constrained by the expectations that came with being in such a committed relationship at a young age. This experience was a pivotal moment in my personal development, as it forced me to grapple with questions of independence, identity, and the nature of love and commitment.

Through these challenges, I discovered my own resilience and capacity for growth. I learned the importance of communication, compromise, and understanding—lessons that have profoundly shaped who I am today. Our relationship, though it eventually ended, was far from a failure. It was a significant chapter in my life, filled with valuable lessons and beautiful memories that have left a lasting impact.

Together, we brought two amazing children into the world, who have been a source of immense joy and purpose. Raising them has been one of the most rewarding experiences of my life. Their unique personalities and achievements have brought pride and happiness to our family. Now, as they have grown and started families of their own, seeing our family expand with three wonderful grandchildren has been an incredible blessing. Watching our children become loving and responsible parents has filled my heart with gratitude and pride.

Despite the end of our romantic relationship, our bond as co-parents has remained strong. We have always prioritized our children's well-being, which has allowed us to maintain a healthy and respectful partnership. This mutual respect has not only strengthened our co-parenting relationship but has also fostered a close-knit and supportive family environment.

Our shared commitment to our family has ensured that our children and grandchildren are surrounded by love and support, creating a strong foundation for future generations.

Reflecting on this time, I see it as a period of immense personal growth and transformation. It was a time when I often felt adrift, disconnected from my spiritual path and more preoccupied with the material aspects of life. My concerns centered around career achievements, social status, and the approval of others, which often left me feeling spiritually empty. These distractions pulled me away from the deeper, more meaningful aspects of my faith. However, as I navigated these experiences, I began to realize that they were not obstacles, but opportunities for growth. Each challenge and setback served as a lesson, pushing me to look inward and question my priorities. It was through these struggles that I found a renewed sense of faith. I came to understand that faith is not merely a set of beliefs or rituals; it is a profound source of strength and guidance, providing clarity and purpose in the midst of life's chaos. This journey has been a cornerstone of my spiritual and personal awakening, teaching me to embrace the uncertainties of life with a deeper trust in God's plan.

This chapter of my life was a pivotal period that deeply influenced my journey toward self-discovery and fulfillment. The significant age difference between my children's father and me brought unique challenges and perspectives. It pushed me to mature quickly, as I navigated the complexities of being in a relationship with someone older and more experienced. The circumstances we faced, including the social and economic pressures of our situation, forced me to confront and appreciate the value of life experiences and the wisdom they impart.

I began to understand that personal growth often involves recognizing when certain situations or relationships no longer serve our best interests. It became clear that it's not only acceptable but necessary to outgrow certain aspects of our lives to continue evolving. This realization was both liberating and daunting, as it meant making tough decisions and sometimes walking away from people or environments that had once felt safe or familiar.

Throughout this time, I continually learned more about myself — my strengths, my values, and my aspirations. I gained a clearer understanding of what I wanted from life, both for myself and my children. This period was a critical part of my journey, shaping my identity and setting the stage for the future I envisioned.

In sharing this story, I hope to inspire others to reflect on their own journeys with a positive outlook and to recognize the significance of every moment. Every experience, whether challenging or joyous, contributes to our growth and understanding, shaping who we are and how we view the world. There's no perfect guide to life, but the teachings in the Bible and the lessons we learn along the way offer invaluable guidance and comfort. They remind us that we are not alone in our struggles and triumphs, and that there is wisdom to be gained from both our successes and our setbacks.

I encourage everyone to take time to document their experiences, no matter how ordinary they may seem. Writing down your story is a powerful way to reflect on your past, gain clarity about your present, and envision your future. It allows you to see patterns, recognize growth, and appreciate the moments that have shaped you. Even the smallest details can hold profound meaning, and capturing them in writing helps to preserve your memories and insights.

Moreover, sharing our stories with others is a way to connect, inspire, and uplift each other. It reminds us that we are all capable of growth, resilience, and finding joy in the journey. By being open about our experiences, we create a sense of community and understanding, helping others see that they are not alone in their struggles and that they too can overcome challenges. In this way, our stories become a testament to the human spirit and a source of encouragement for all who read them.

Chapter 9
Friends and Fun Times

    Let me take you back to one of the most exhilarating periods of my life, an era when the nightlife pulsed with a unique vibrancy and the air itself seemed charged with electric energy. This was a time when the city's heartbeat was synchronized with the rhythm of its nightclubs and the allure of live entertainment. Imagine walking into a club, where the music didn't just play—it enveloped you, every beat reverberating through your body as you moved to its infectious tempo. The atmosphere was intoxicating, with neon lights casting a kaleidoscope of colors across the dance floor and the air thick with the scent of anticipation and excitement. The nights were long and endless, with clubs remaining open until the early hours of the morning—often until 7 AM—creating a backdrop where music, dancing, and revelry seamlessly intertwined. Each visit felt like an escape into a world where the boundaries of reality blurred, and every moment was filled with the promise of adventure and connection. The city was alive, and with each night, it beckoned you to dive deeper into its realm of boundless energy and exhilarating possibilities.

    In this exhilarating chapter of my life, I found myself working for MCI, a leading telecommunications company known for its long-distance telephone services. This was a time when making a long-distance call was a luxury, with charges meticulously calculated by the minute, a far cry from the instant and cost-free communication we experience today. MCI was at the forefront of this industry, pioneering the way people connected across great distances. My role at MCI not only afforded me a sense of financial independence and stability but also opened doors to a realm of entertainment and experiences that I might have otherwise missed. It was within the bustling atmosphere of MCI that I encountered a diverse and remarkable group of individuals. These connections proved to be pivotal, as many of these extraordinary people would go on to play significant roles in both my personal and professional life. Their influence and camaraderie enriched my journey, creating lasting bonds that continue to shape my path.

    Among these exceptional friends was RL, a person whose presence was nothing short of unforgettable. From the moment you met him, RL's vibrant personality was immediately apparent, radiating a magnetic charm that drew people in effortlessly. He had a remarkable ability to light up any room, seamlessly blending humor and charisma in every interaction. RL's enthusiasm for life was infectious, and he had a special knack for captivating an audience with his quick wit and engaging stories.

    RL's reputation as a ladies' man was well-known, but there was so much more to him than his flirtatious exterior. Behind the playful banter and charismatic facade was an individual with an extraordinary gift for cooking. His culinary talents were unparalleled; every dish he prepared was a masterpiece, meticulously crafted with a blend of creativity and skill. His culinary creations were not just meals but experiences, transforming our gatherings into memorable feasts that everyone eagerly anticipated.

DON'T HATE

Despite RL's move to Puerto Rico, where he now courageously confronts a challenging battle with cancer, his legacy endures. The joy and warmth he brought into our lives continue to resonate deeply. RL's influence remains a cherished part of our memories, a testament to the lasting impact he made on those fortunate enough to know him.

Then there was Ann, a vibrant and vivacious friend whose zest for life perfectly matched my own enthusiasm for the entertainment industry. Ann was not just a companion but a co-adventurer in our shared passion for the glitz and glamour of the entertainment scene. Together, we explored the pulsating nightlife of exclusive clubs, mingled with celebrities at glittering events, and reveled in the electric atmosphere that defined the high-society parties we frequented. Her infectious energy and charisma transformed every outing into an unforgettable experience. Whether we were attending a star-studded gala, navigating the intricate social circles of Hollywood, or simply enjoying a night out in the city, Ann's presence added a unique sparkle to every moment. Despite her recent move to North Carolina, which took her away from the bustling scene we once shared, our friendship has remained a steadfast and cherished part of my life. We continue to bridge the miles between us through regular updates, heartfelt conversations, and mutual support, celebrating each other's successes and providing comfort through life's inevitable ups and downs.

My tenure at MCI was marked not only by significant professional advancement but also by profound personal fulfillment. The company's work culture and flexible hours provided an ideal framework for me to pursue my passion for the vibrant nightlife scene. The clubs and venues we frequented had operating hours that began in the early evening and extended into the early hours of the morning, creating a seamless synergy with my work schedule. This harmonious balance allowed me to excel in my career while indulging in my love for the nightlife, which included everything from high-energy dance floors to intimate live music performances. The duality of this experience was incredibly enriching; it afforded me financial stability and a rich tapestry of social and cultural experiences. The nights out not only served as a form of relaxation and entertainment but also as a source of inspiration and connection, further enhancing my overall quality of life.

In those days, attending a live event was the quintessential way to immerse oneself in the spellbinding world of celebrity performances. Before the era of social media, where every glance, gesture, and moment can be instantly shared and broadcast to a global audience, witnessing a performance in person was a rare and treasured experience. The absence of smartphones and digital cameras meant that the only way to savor these fleeting moments was to be physically present, heightening the sense of exclusivity and magic. Each event was an unparalleled adventure, a chance to be part of a singular, unrepeatable experience that was woven into the fabric of memory. The palpable energy of the crowd, the thrill of anticipation, and the shared sense of excitement made each night out an extraordinary journey, marked by the collective awe and admiration of those fortunate enough to witness the live spectacle firsthand.

As the years have rolled by, RL and Ann have embarked on new and transformative journeys that have reshaped their lives in profound ways. RL's relocation to the vibrant shores of Puerto Rico marked the beginning of a significant chapter for him, one filled with both challenges and opportunities. Amidst this major transition, he faced a formidable adversary in the form of cancer, a battle that tested his courage and resilience. His unwavering strength through this ordeal became a testament to his indomitable spirit. Despite these life-altering events, the essence of our bond has endured with remarkable steadfastness.

Our friendship has continued to flourish as we have supported each other through life's vicissitudes. We often find ourselves reminiscing about the treasured moments we've shared, and one particularly poignant example of our enduring connection was a heartwarming reunion at Myrtle Beach. This gathering, held over the Fourth of July weekend, was more than just a casual get-together; it was a celebration of our shared history and the joy we have found in each other's company over the years. We stayed at a charming resort, where the sound of the waves and the gentle sea breeze provided a fitting backdrop for our festivities. The highlight of our reunion was watching an awe-inspiring display of fireworks lighting up the night sky, a vivid reminder of the joy and camaraderie that have always marked our time together. We indulged in a sumptuous feast of snow crab legs, a nod to our past adventures and a tribute to the many good times we've experienced. Each moment was a celebration of our enduring friendship and a reaffirmation of the bond that has remained strong despite the changing tides of our lives.

These reunions and ongoing connections underscore the profound and enduring value of true friendship. Despite the physical distance that may separate us, the essence of our bond remains steadfast and unbroken. Whether through heartfelt conversations, long phone calls, or shared experiences, we manage to bridge the miles that lie between us, making it feel as though no time has passed since our last meeting. Friends like RL and Ann are intricately woven into the fabric of my life, their influence and companionship enriching my journey in ways that are both subtle and profound. Each interaction, whether it's a spontaneous chat or a deeply reflective exchange, reaffirms the strength of our connection and the mutual understanding that binds us together. Their presence, even from afar, continues to provide warmth and perspective, highlighting the timeless and invaluable nature of genuine friendship.

Reflecting on this chapter, it's clear that friendships and shared moments of joy have played a crucial role in shaping my narrative. The bonds formed during these times have been more than just fleeting experiences; they have provided a sense of adventure and camaraderie that infused my life with vibrancy and meaning. The nights spent in laughter, the spontaneous adventures, and the profound conversations have all contributed to a rich tapestry of memories that color my story. These friendships have not only been a source of joy but also a reminder of the importance of nurturing and valuing the connections we build with those who matter most. As we navigate the future, it is these cherished relationships and the experiences we've shared that truly enrich our lives, making each chapter of our journey resonate with unforgettable significance.

Chapter 10
Staying True to Yourself

In a world overflowing with diverse opinions and relentless judgments, it frequently seems as if our personal journeys are obscured by a cloud of negativity and external pressures. These forces can manifest in various ways, from overt criticism and unsolicited advice to subtle societal expectations that challenge our self-worth. Despite this overwhelming barrage, it is essential to recognize that remaining authentic to oneself in the face of such adversity is not only attainable but immensely fulfilling. This chapter delves into the transformative power of embracing positivity, nurturing faith, and practicing self-love. By doing so, we can navigate through the stormy seas of criticism and disdain with resilience and grace. Embracing these values offers a beacon of hope and a pathway to inner strength, allowing us to maintain our true essence and find genuine satisfaction amid the chaos.

The Power of Faith and Prayer

In the complex journey of navigating life's emotional turbulence, faith and prayer stand out as profound sources of strength and solace. For many, including myself, prayer becomes more than just a ritual—it transforms into a sanctuary where we can offload our burdens, seek guidance, and establish a deep connection with a higher power. This sacred practice not only offers a refuge from the storms of daily life but also provides a wellspring of inner strength and spiritual calm, essential for managing our emotions effectively.

When faced with overwhelming negative feelings or the sting of external judgment, I turn to prayer as a grounding force. In these moments of distress, prayer allows me to center my thoughts and emotions, offering a reminder that divine love and guidance are constants in my life. By focusing on this higher connection, I find the strength to overcome feelings of anger or resentment, replacing them with peace and compassion. This transformation is not instantaneous but evolves through consistent practice, where each prayer reinforces a sense of trust in the divine plan.

Prayer also plays a crucial role in fostering self-love and self-understanding. It serves as a mirror reflecting my innermost values and beliefs, guiding me to align my actions with my moral compass. This alignment encourages a more empathetic and kinder approach toward others, reinforcing the idea that our interactions can reflect our spiritual state. As my spiritual practice deepens, I find my perspective on life evolving significantly. The practice of prayer shifts my view, making it easier to navigate through negativity with a heart full of love and compassion.

Moreover, the act of prayer is a continuous dialogue with the divine, offering not only requests for help but also expressions of gratitude and acknowledgment of the positive aspects of life. This dialogue enriches my spiritual journey, cultivating a deeper sense of gratitude and mindfulness. It allows me to recognize and appreciate the small blessings and moments of joy that might otherwise go unnoticed amidst life's chaos.

In essence, prayer is a dynamic practice that transforms emotional challenges into opportunities for spiritual growth. It helps me cultivate resilience, maintain a sense of inner peace, and approach life's difficulties with a heart open to love and understanding. Through faith and prayer, I am reminded of a higher purpose and connection, which provides both comfort and strength in the face of adversity.

Embracing Positivity Through Self-Awareness

Staying positive amidst life's adversities often begins with a profound sense of self-awareness. At its core, self-awareness involves a deep understanding of our own values, needs, and the ways we interact with others. One crucial aspect of this self-awareness is recognizing how we wish to be treated and using that understanding as a guiding principle in our interactions.

In my journey toward maintaining a positive mindset, I've discovered that the way we treat others profoundly impacts our own emotional state and overall perspective. By adhering to the principle of treating others with the same respect and kindness that we desire in return, we lay the foundation for a constructive and uplifting environment. This approach is not merely about politeness; it's a deliberate practice of empathy and compassion.

When I approach interactions with a mindset of respect, I create a reciprocal dynamic where kindness and understanding flow both ways. This not only enhances my well-being but also fosters a more positive and harmonious atmosphere in all my relationships. It's a simple yet powerful way to nurture positivity in everyday life.

Words possess an extraordinary power—they can either uplift and inspire or wound and demoralize. The language we use and the actions we take have significant effects on those around us. By consciously choosing to speak with positivity and act with compassion, we contribute to an environment where mutual respect and understanding can thrive. This conscious choice to promote positivity through our words and deeds is essential in creating and sustaining a supportive social sphere.

An integral component of self-awareness is the recognition of how judgment and criticism impact both ourselves and others. I have learned that criticism, whether directed outward or inward, often reflects more about the critic than the recipient. When we are quick to judge or criticize, it can create a cycle of negativity that affects our own emotional state and the well-being of those around us.

To counteract this tendency, I focus on fostering a mindset centered around service and improvement. Rather than critiquing others, I seek to understand their perspectives and offer constructive support. This shift from criticism to constructive engagement helps break the cycle of negativity and contributes to a more positive and collaborative environment.

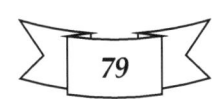

By emphasizing service and improvement—both personally and within my community—I cultivate a cycle of positivity that ultimately benefits everyone involved. When we approach challenges and interactions with a focus on uplifting and supporting one another, we create an environment where positive actions and attitudes are reciprocated.

In essence, embracing positivity through self-awareness is about aligning our actions with our values, choosing to speak and act with kindness, and recognizing the broader impact of judgment and criticism. By doing so, we not only enhance our own sense of well-being but also contribute to a more positive and harmonious world.

The Ripple Effect of Positivity

A key aspect of staying true to oneself lies in recognizing the profound impact our actions and attitudes have on the world around us. Our behaviors and responses not only shape our immediate environment but also set a precedent for how others interact with us and each other. When we approach life with a positive attitude and a genuine willingness to help others, we cultivate a culture where kindness and support become the norm. This nurturing environment can inspire others to mirror these values in their own interactions, creating a ripple effect of goodwill.

Consider a situation where we encounter judgment or hostility. If we respond with love and compassion rather than retaliation or bitterness, we contribute to a more harmonious and supportive atmosphere. Such responses can help diffuse tension and foster an environment where understanding and empathy are more readily embraced. This shift in approach has the potential to interrupt cycles of negativity and violence, paving the way for a more constructive and empathetic culture.

Moreover, it's crucial to understand that maintaining a positive outlook doesn't equate to ignoring problems or pretending that everything is flawless. Instead, positivity involves approaching challenges with a mindset geared toward growth and resolution. By facing difficulties with an open heart and a balanced perspective, we can address issues more effectively and contribute to meaningful change. This approach not only benefits our own lives but also positively impacts those around us, reinforcing a collective effort toward improvement and understanding.

A Call to Action: Moving Beyond Hate

In a world where gun violence and hatred have become alarmingly prevalent, it is crucial now more than ever to advocate for meaningful and transformative change. The increasing frequency of violent acts and the deepening divides in our society call for a concerted effort to challenge these negative forces. By embodying the principles of love, empathy, and faith, we can counteract the detrimental impact of violence and division. It is my sincere hope that this book serves as a beacon of hope and a clarion call for those who are eager to transform both their own lives and their communities.

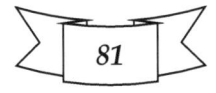

Hatred and hostility often provoke immediate and emotional reactions. However, responding with anger or violence only serves to perpetuate the cycle of negativity. It is essential to recognize that such reactions do not resolve conflicts or heal wounds but instead escalate the cycle of retaliation and suffering. Instead, we must strive to rise above these challenges by remaining steadfast in our values and embracing a path of peace and understanding. This approach not only uplifts ourselves but also sets an example for others to follow, fostering a culture of reconciliation rather than discord.

To navigate through hostility with grace and effectiveness, we need to anchor ourselves in our core principles of compassion and empathy. By prioritizing these values, we can turn adverse situations into opportunities for growth and connection. Every act of kindness, every effort to understand others' perspectives, and every commitment to peaceful dialogue contributes to breaking down the barriers of hatred. Through these actions, we have the power to inspire those around us to adopt similar principles, creating ripples of positive change that extend far beyond our immediate circles.

In conclusion, remaining true to oneself amidst criticism and hate is not merely a personal endeavor but a collective effort towards building a more compassionate world. It is through faith, self-awareness, and positive action that we can gracefully navigate life's challenges. Our journey towards a fulfilling life is deeply intertwined with our ability to stay authentic, spread love, and remain steadfast in our commitment to positivity and self-growth. It is through this commitment that we foster a more understanding and harmonious society.

Thank you for taking the time to engage with this chapter. I hope it inspires you to embrace love, reject hatred, and remain true to yourself. May God's love and peace guide us through every step of our journey, illuminating our path with hope and grace.

Made in the USA
Columbia, SC
20 October 2024